AF490837

Phoenix 5

The Lives of the Phoenix

Phraxen

On Zolidous the planet of the Gods, where everyone has abilities, Phraxen the Son of the great and mighty Kronos. A young Man that is next in line to command the Zilodian army. The problem is Respect is earned, and they see him as privileged, a brat, someone that didn't earn his marks.

Little does his people know, Kronos is Harder on his children then anyone under command. Phraxen and his brothers were turned on each other but mostly against the youngest.

He'd be tortured by their powers, drowned to death and brought back, electrocuted, and the list of abilities goes on. But because you need to be at age to get your powers, he couldn't defend himself.

It's different for all zilodians everyone gets

their powers at various ages. Normally it's when they accept who they are, good or pure evil.

Phraxen for years was a joke to his fathers army. Until 1 year, they were attacking the enemy army and became trapped in the under ground caverns. Hundreds of creatures call it home, the Medusa, Hydra, cyclopes, cerberus, the list goes on.

After several years of them fighting for their lives to survive, the army survives and Phraxen earns his place as their leader. Earning his abilities, him and Kronos become mortal enemies. The war tears their planet in half.

Phraxen Becomes just like his Father, a blood thirsty dictator. He becomes intrigued with time travel, his friend Orins ability. Eventually a space storm with the ability to eliminate the planet is detected several years in advance, before anyone else.

With help from the zilodian rogues, he's able to Clone himself an others that may not survive the destruction. Phraxen grew to regret his actions and saw the storm as a way out.

By the time his plans were revealed. It was

too late. Anyone with the powers to survive deep space and make it too a nearby planet did. They Called the planet Olympus.

The Phraxen clone was discovered and adopted, not knowing who is was.

Thus beginning The Untold Mystery of The Phoenix.

Gabriel

The young man that could barely say hi, or interact with those of his village, no one thought he'd be anything in life. Gabriel a trained fighter, some survival skills, but very little real world knowledge. With his Friends Malter, Shalna, Raylo, Nailia and Ralam, the world would stand no chance.

He started his life search at 17 years old. After fighting his brothers Zeus, Poseidon and Hades. Gabriel went back to earth.. In an odd way.
Now out of his time, at 25 the 1st few years he spends his days talking to his friends from the past in the tunnels.

In the tunnels he can meet with his friends, but they cannot leave when not in their time. Gabriel is in the future, his people are in the past, he can't go back to his old life and they cannot join him.

A-ra: How have you been?

Gabriel: Sad...... I miss you guys... badly.

A-ra: I miss you …

Gabriel: There's so much beauty here, the land is untouched. I wish I could show you. (As soon as he says it, a drone appears and scans his mind, it relays the images in his head.)

A-ra: This is what you're seeing?! This is amazing.

Gabriel: Hows Freedom city?

A-ra: Well... see for yourself. (the cities progress is shown)

Gabriel: Everyone is working together finally.

A-ra: After what you did, how could they not?

Gabriel: It's in humans nature to screw things up.

A-ra: I didn't say there weren't problems.

Like before you came back to our time. We fought the fozicon war... that took a lot of lives.

Gabriel: What happened?

A-ra: Ralam happened. He brought everyone together, and they killed all of the frozicons at once. Pretty ingenious. Anything trickling in to you? You are in our future right?

Gabriel: I am but..... I've traveled the planet, no one lives here except 2 other people.

A-ra: Have you talked to them?

Gabriel: No, I chose to stay away ...

A-ra: Oh... ok...

Gabriel: How are the others?

A-ra: I know it's been a while, They're very busy.

Gabriel: I get it... It's not something I'm happy with.... we all need to move on.

A-ra: You really mean that? Because,

well..... us here, alone..

Gabriel: I get it! Haha. You're making me blush..... but I can't go in your time and you can't in mine... If you get pregnant, What's to say the kid can come to either time?

A-ra: It could walk In both times, thus we have a way to be together.

Gabriel: I really wish it worked that way. But in order for us to cross into each others time. We need enough power.

A-ra: Absorb some power from the sun, or surrounding stars.

Gabriel: I tried that... I'd need that space storm. I searched for the next one..... I thought maybe since I'm so far into the future another one would come.

A-ra: So? Anything?

Gabriel: (Yells) SERFROXY!!

Serfroxy: Here sir!

Gabriel: Bring up Data please.

Serfroxy:		Data shows that a storm has indeed come and gone, and there is no data currently of another.

Gabriel:		Could I simply time travel to the storm that passed?

Serfroxy:		No you could not, for that storm was used to reshape earth after its extermination. It happened a million years ago.

A-ra:		What? So that's it? Wait...... Earth is still in danger then..

Gabriel:	That won't happen until even your 5th generation is long dead.

A-ra:		Can you tell me when My Earth will die?

Serfroxy:		It will not happen for several thousand years.

A-ra:		What about his time.

Gabriel:	I"d rather not know. I want to make the future, not be told what it is. Also I think we need to slow our meeting.

A-ra: Why??

Gabriel: Because we're hurting ourselves by doing this.

A-ra: Is this what you actually want?

Gabriel: No.... But.

A /.m-ra: (Mad at 1st but then gets it) We can at least talk face to face sometimes...

Gabriel: It's better is we just stop.

A-ra: Fine, I'll always love you.

Gabriel: I'll always love you.

Before he starts, Gabriel journeys out again, before he just used the tunnels to get around the planet for recon. This time is to really look at his new world, He's seen Earth before on his journey, but that was war. Gabriel is in a different time and might as well be an entirely different planet.

Every thing is changed, remembering where the land marks he's visited in the past, he sees how different the land is. The area where his village was, you'd never of guessed it was even there. Gladiator arenas, nothing. Eventually animals are seen. And they're amazing creatures. It's fully understood now that he's not home anymore.

Gabriel goes to work, figuring out how to bring his brethren there and start their world all over. plans for years. After he triggers the becon, the Zilodians arrive. They live out their lives on Earth where mythology is then born.

Vernon

A man with a family, wonderful wife, 3 daughters. Vernon with the life that most would dream of, fame and fortune. A deal in his business went bad, the partners blamed him. They sent men to his house and killed the family in front of him.

His screams unlocked his potential and he burns all of them alive. Not long after, 3 other men find him. And reveal they're his brothers. Somehow he just knows and understands.

They go to his massive building and with his fire, and the powers of thunder, water and Death. Everyone is killed. A digital message the thunder brother sends to the world, exposes the crimes his partners blamed him for.

After that day, the 4 keep taking down the corrupt elites, to change the world for the better.

Alto

A war veteran that was thrown away by his country, left to rot in the ally's of his home town. Kicked out of every park he goes to, til one day his anger gets out of control

Alto goes to a major news outlet and voices his opinion. The 3 block radius is incinerated and only he walks out alive, the question is, how?

Alto: What's happening to me? How did I do that?

He has this feeling to go to the nearby military base, he has old friends that are high up the chain that take pity on him.

Bill: Do you want to see something top secret?

Alto: Wont that get you in trouble?

Bill: I'll dock my pay later. (Walks him through the base giving the tour. And they get to the great surprise.)

Alto:	So what it's a door?

Bill:	Thing about that is, scientist's all over the planet have scanned enough parts of the earth to create a map. Doors like this are everywhere,

Alto:	What's in them?

Bill:	That's the interesting part... No one knows, no one has been able to get in.

Alto:	Why set up a base around them?

Bill:	Simple curiosity, if it's locked, there's a good reason. But it has a palm scanner, so we know it does open.

Alto:	You mean you added one to open it?

Bill:	No, it was already on. Why don't you try it, evey one else on this base and beyond has.. Go ahead.

	The rugged, scared, grey haired 55 year old vet nervously walks up to the door. Not knowing what's going to happen, places his hand on the scanner.. Like with everyone else.... nothing.. he starts walking away, when it opens like an elevator door.

Everyone surrounding jumps in their skin, Bill orders Alto away but he goes closer, being drawn in. He walks through and soldiers try to follow but they're stopped by a barrier, even Bill try's and nothing.

Even though he's confused, Alto keeps walking down the strange blue lit path. It leads to a pitch black opening that lights up once inside.

Where a man walks up to him, one long pointed ear, the other cut from an old war wound, blue genes, and a gray and black hoodie, brown hair with blue patches. He explains everything

Altos life changes after that. Learning his powers and assisting the military to eliminate threats. They turn on him eventually, but when it's humans vs a God....

His life cycle takes him through several human generations, until the next Phoenix is born.

Mayvor

A child of 10 years old, biggest worry in the world is if Ma-ya likes him or not. His village is small, 400 people. His parents are very relaxed with Mayvor to the point its like they don't care, he comes and goes from the village as he pleases.

Outside is a chaotic mess, a fallen world with in what use to be paradise. Amazing creatures such as only exists in fairy tales. Such a beautiful world, ruined by mans greed and hatred.

The Boy likes to go out and play with the animals which are very innocent, until threatened.

Mayvor plays with Ma-ya in their little park. Tagging each other, jumping on equipment they have. When she asks.

Ma-ya: Do you like me?

Mayvor: (Caught off guard by the question.)
What? What makes you ask?

Ma-ya: Well, a lot of my friends tell me they
notice you looking at me and saying so. If you do
that's ok, I just want to know from you.

Mayvor: Yes I like you. Do you like me?

Ma-ya: You're always nice to me, when the
other boys are mean.. I like that..

Mayvor: I just don't like people being mean to
people I enjoy.

     Both kids deal with their fair share of
bullying, and are just tired of it. Going to school
it's something of a chore for both of them, a few
more too. A small group of boys and girls love to
pick on classmates, the adults could careless and
side it as kids being kids.

     The boys start to beat on Mayvor, while a
few other kids are as well. Adults are no where to
be found.

     He feels helpless and alone, no one to help
or care. The boy feels a rush of energy and
power. Mayvor gets up, tossing the kids that are

beating on him to the side, His eyes light up with fire, and voice is enough to give any adult nightmares.

Mayvor: Leave us, alone!!!

The kids run away for their lives to tell their parents, obviously no one believes them. Ma-ya gives him a kiss on his cheek and big hug.

Even though he harnessed the power of the Phoenix, he couldn't summon it at will, his emotions had to be out of control to work. Mayvor and his friends weren't close before that event, but afterwards, inseparable. They would grow up to be the strongest in their land, defending anyone too weak to fight off the strong.

It's not until 10 years later he discovers the truth behind his powers.

Scepter

A man with everything, the ruler of his world, he came to this stature using his abilities. Coming to his powers at the age of 20, using them to force control over his civilization. Nothing was able to stop him.

Once Scepter found out that he can create and manipulate fire, he tested his limits and got stronger. Gaining experience by attacking those that irritate him, up to police, and higher. Eventually he gets greedy and pushes for political power, not to run, but to kill.

All military forces attempt to attack, but are slaughtered. It took him a few years to gain his strengthen, now at 22 his obey or die plan runs the span of a year. Apparently it's not easy to over throw a government, you can't just knock on the door and say. "Yeah if you don't mind, I'm taking over now, if that's ok with you."

Scepter became the ruler of earth by eliminating any one that came to challenge him. Even his brethren tried, others with powers, he just grew to powerful.

He discovered the tunnel system and was dealt with

Taylor

A young women fighting the abuse of a time that's obsolete. Rights that belong to everyone is being limited to sex. Taylor slowly finds this out. In a time before technology, and before equality is for everyone, she learns just how dark the world is.

Men treat her like trash, use, manipulate, rape and abuse her for years. By the time she meets a guy worth anything, she doesn't trust it, and pushes him away as if he's like every man that did her wrong.

One day the person she blew off tries to save her from being raped, unfortunately the situation triggers her abilities to come out. This releases a fiery shock wave that kills anyone around her.

Scared and confused, she runs until she reaches a forest. Here she finds a natural time pocket that's with in a few trees. The electrical field around it prevents animals from running in.

Not knowing it's there, Taylor runs right through it, and crosses paths with another life.

Mer-Lek

How long? A few million years, give or take. Where? Well that's a story.

My name is Mer-Lek, and I am a Phoenix. My powers were activated the day our world went into chaos. Images from other people I've never met flooded my brain. Names I don't know. Adventures that blew my mind.

I gained their experience, and used it. While my world was burning, I took advantage and played around with it. As people were dying, the military was struggling to keep control. And I made sure they lost it.

Soldiers trying to kill innocent people, children even, abusing their power. I Phoenix up and defend the defenseless. The problem was I couldn't stop, I kept going until I leveled all hostels. In the process i took out the entire worlds defense.

All of this took a few years. Until I became board and started planet jumping. Using the stars to travel, I couldn't get enough of the killing. Many planets I went too, I took down the major command.

Then it finally happened. An army of a space criminal force found me, I was taken to the most famous prison in existence..

Main Prison Guard: To all of you space scum, I'd like to give you a big warm welcome.. Welcome to TARTARUS, the most deadliest and inescapable prison ever created! Most of you have abilities, that's fantastic, because here, you're basic. How is that possible? I will tell you how. Everyone in this prison has a nanite fluid in them that disables their powers. So good luck killing us! Hahaha! Now get the F*** out of here!!

This Prison is not messing around, the security measures are overkill. Guards, androids, turrets, even the nanite fluid. So escaping will be fun.

    With all of these precautions, there's still always a way. I'm placed into the community, and its all glares... not a good sign. 4 Aliens stand in front of me, large teal with big bulky arms and long fingers with sharp claws. Small purple with skin dreads..... and long tail. And 2 surviving Adversi from the old great cleansing.

    I put up a good fight..... no that's a lie I was laid out instantly and placed in my cell.

Probsni: Soooo... The new Phoenix.... hows that working out?

Mer-Lek: I'm Mer-Lek... Who are you?

Probsni: Probsni, good to meet you. I'm one of your brothers.

Mer-Lek: What kind of name is that? And I have no... wait.... Your Poseidon?

Probsni: Ding....... Ding we have a winner. Oh and the others are here.

Mer-Lek: Freaking amazing.

Next what they call day in this dump, we go into the activity area. Its a boring big room that has day, night and weather simulations. And there are the 4 that laid me out... great, they want a 2nd round.

My brothers lay them out fast, then convo.

Hate-es: So your the new phoenix, I'm Hate-es that's Hate and then seperation mark and ES.

Mer-Lek: And your past name was Hades......

Hate-es: How do you know that?

Probsni: He remembers.

Zeuk: I'm Zeuk.

Mer-Lek: Mer-Lek... Wow your names aren't original at all..

Zeuk: How do you remember us?

Mer-Lek: I............... Remember

everything, about all of my lives. Like how I killed all of you back when I was Gabriel. How do you guys always survive? I'm curious about that. Only I have the ability to reincarnate.

Probsni: You're not the only smart one in the family.

Hate-es: Now that we're together.... Lets get out of this place.

Mer-Lek: Yeah but problem is, no powers, and as you saw I suck at fighting without them.

Zeuk: Well, you've always had a nak for defying the ods.. That Gabriel life, you were a major pain in our butt! And the most resilient. Some how, You're always able to get your powers back.

Probsni: Every day there's a gladiator battle. We know you. Get going enough and you can override the nanite slug.

Hate-es: The only thing we need to do is get them to choose you for the fight.. luckily, they love fresh meat.

Mer-Lek: Fun time.

　　　We go through our day, meal time, or what they consider a meal... some space garbage. And then our jobs..... my brothers were right on the gladiator thing.. I almost didn't make day 1 and it was all to obvious. And yes I got too much crap for that.

Zeuk: What the hell was that?

Hate-es: Bro, even Aphrodite fights better then you.

Mer-Lek: I do remember leading with that I can't fight.... I have a 2nd today, I'll do better.

　　　During the fights I see Images from my Gabriel life. Ralam talking crap for most of the fight, and other friends. Shalna and Malter give their comments.

Ralam: So if it isn't the Great and powerful Phoenix!

Mer-Lek: I don't like that tone.

Ralam: And I don't like that my
sacrifice was in vain.

Mer-Lek: I'm a completely different life
you idiot.

Ralam: Yet you're the one yelling to
yourself, in the middle of a battle.

        My foe is standing in front of me very
confused. I kill him winning the fight and the
crowd, the guards love my style, it to excite
everyone else as well.

        In the prison yard.

Zeuk: You have a plan I can tell.

Hate-es: Spill it it fire breather.

Mer-lek: Says the fiery god of death.. Yes I
have a plan next fight.

Zeuk: Good, keep the details to yourself.

Mer-lek: They're Listening?

Hate-es: You never know when they are.

Mer-lek: Did the yard change?

Prob-sni: Yes you idiot, the layout randomly switches around to throw us off.

Mer-lek: Smart.

Zeuk: How are you the smartest of us again?

Mer-lek: Tell me again how I killed all of you as Gabriel again? Oh yeah, I figured out how to clone, time travel regain who I was and took all of you on at the same time, then find out all of you were being played by credon..... no response? Yeah... I figured...

I take my time with the escape. Learn the changes and every possible layout. If you're not looking, of course its random. I figured out how to hack the security bots.... they're now programmed on my voice to attack who I say. It's time now to act.... but I still can't access my powers without death.. best I could to was hack a system delay.

It's time for my fight it's the Adversi they gang up on me and I give them a good run, but don't kill them, there's no need. Then..

Mer-lek: Bots, Kill the Guards!!

As they're distracted, I fight m way through and get the serum that counteracts what they gave us. Abilities activated... I give it to my brothers and we burn the prison to the ground.

Alot of prisoners are killed because of the liquid chips in them. Only a few dozen are smart enough to avoid fighting before getting rid of the killer chip in them. With that said, the different abilities from the many aliens are impressive.

Zeuk: Haha, now we own Tartarus... Nice.

Mer-lek: Ok dipshits time to go to earth and take the tunnels.

Jacob

A fire fighter with amazing instincts, He never found out he was the Phoenix. Barely knew he had powers. But his friends always knew he was special. His ability to know fire, what its doing, and small scale controlling it.

Jacob only had basic abilities to the point he was human. Fire didn't have an effect on his skin much, but could low key talk to it.

Because his powers were weak, he was incinerated at the end.

The Original

My Zolidous name is Phraxen, My Human name is Paul. I met him once, Gabriel that is. We were lost in time, and came back to my time of 2020. I helped him get to the point he needed to be.

What I didn't tell him.... Is I'm the one that made him in the 1st place. The space storm eliminated my planet.. the strongest survived, I barely made it out alive.

People don't think planets can have a soul... but I saw it...as the ionic powers of the storm ripped through Zolidous, and I could see it... next thing I know... I'm on a beach but it's not a real beach...down the sides I can see others. People going through their own test In life.

That's when I see her.

Zelory: You're awake... That's good...

Paul: Who are you?

Zelory: I am Zelory... I saved you from the explosion.

Paul: Where are we?

Zelory: You don't like the beach? Well I thought it would be good for you to transition out of.

Paul: Where am I really?

Zelory: On a planet a few galaxies away.

Paul: What? Who are you? A person from here?

Zelory: No...... I am your planet.....

Paul: How is that even close to possible?

Zelory: The storm.. It changed me...

Paul: To what?

Zelory: One of you I think.... I was only able to save a group of you, I had to becareful. This form is new to me, I'm learning what I can do.

Paul: Take me out of this please, I want to see who I'm with.

       We pan out and see our surroundings. It's a beautiful planet that she chose to set us. The survivors are my friends and a few others. We decide to make a life on the new planet. Zelory Learns what she can do. Which is pretty much anything.

       She learns how to give life through the energy around. We're a small group that sticks close together. But even the closest friends fall out some times.

       Zelory and I stayed with each other and traveled, everywhere. Galaxies, planets, space and time itself. With her I could be anywhere at any time, that also means any age I want.

       This power is used to turn Earth into an underground timeless lair.
The Tunnels.... I built them to be a home despite time, an anchor for not just myself but for all versions of me and my allies. This structure spans the entire planet. Yes civilizations have worked hard to get in, many came close. But not one success.

We influence civilizations, leaders. I'd be lying if I said I didn't use our powers for personal gain. What kind of immortals would we be if we didn't have the resources to back it up? I'm always updating the tunnels information to help the others.

We travel far into the future, seeing thousands of civilizations begin and end. Millions of different life forms. The most evil are the different human versions. Creating ways and reasons to hate each other.

I know every one that will become the Phoenix, I have met many of them. Good, evil.. their lives run on for different times. Some a few hundred years, or thousands. Not all of them are exciting. Gabriel was the most special case.

There are many Phoenix versions. Many lives altered by them, for the Good and bad. They are meant to watch and protect. I watch them and help when it's catastrophic.

The Tunnels

Phraxen and the other phoenix's worked on building the network of tunnels throughout the ages. They run into the entire planet. The uses are nearly limitless.

To start with getting in, your DNA needs to be preprogramed into the system. Otherwise you cannot gain access unless someone gives you access.

If you haven't discovered you're a protector, or abilities, the AI challenges you. Survive, you get in don't you die. People that aren't programmed and killed. Traveling the network is simple, anywhere you want to go. Step on a teleporting pad and say the location.

Information look up. The AI's name is Serfroxy anything the user needs, he looks up. The Database is vast. All of the Phoenix's contribute to the archives.

Future tech. There are thousands of gadgets they can use. Time machines that use the users abilities to time travel. They can go as far into the past or future as they want, but they need to have to power to go and return.

The problem Gabriel faced was he absorbed a massive amount of energy, releasing it didn't just send him into the future, but a different dimension. He traveled to 2020 via natural time pocket, But returned to his time because it was only time he was moving through time.

A portable teleporting device, weapons for any purpose. Living sections. Only Phraxen or...... Paul really knows the true abilities of the network..

When the Planet cycles, dies and reforms, the tunnels remain untouched. Any Phoenix or Zolodian can survive. It's not the matter of time traveling to avoid the rebirth of the planet, but the power too. Only some one that can absorb the energy of the liquid rock can skip it, or having the devices channel the power.

The Tunnels are the greatest structure ever created, and can never be matched by anyone on earth.

The Phoenix Process

Everything can be explained.. but until you find the Person or being, or thing that can answer the question. It's a mystery. Can the Phoenix process be ended? Yes. Take away their powers, make them mortal and kill them. But the ability is resilient, yet depends on the persons will to keep going. Many of the versions had their abilities stripped, yet succeeded.

When one dies, another starts, but only when activated. As far as the lives and origin of the Phoenix... that's no longer a Mystery to you.

There are too many lives to talk about, too many stories to get into. Strong and courageous people. Let them be known by their own time. As far as now, You know how the process started, and who started it. Remember their journeys, and heroics.

The Lives of the Phoenix

My Phoenix Journey

From the Author

I wrote The Untold Mystery of the Phoenix 10 years ago. It was the 1st book I've ever written, exciting too. Not being a reader, I had to do my research, read enough books to know I didn't enjoy how they were written. So I made my own way. It took time for me to find my method.

For some reason I was fixated on the Phoenix, so I started to think. When I focus on a story, the ideas flood in. I had the series mapped out right away. The set up I wanted to be fun and inviting, not showing too much action but built slowly.

I joked about how ridiculous the mythology is. My play for the books was to show the real God. At that moment I made Gabriel an atheist. He questions everything about their fire God. And leaves home to find himself and change his world.

It was drawn out I admit that, but that

was needed to tell the details for the 1st. To layout the world, but 2 was to layout the plot.

2 took 8 months to write because I had to break. But it was bigger and badder. I made the characters friends mains as well and gave them a piece of story. I put in more of what I enjoyed. I loved the movie Gladiator, and made Gabriel a fighter.

The land I wanted the end of the world feel, screwed up weather, and ecosystem. The civilization before messed it up and it was spiraling out of control. Sound familiar?

My biggest issue with the series what keeping the details in line, and the motivation to tell the story.

Phoenix 4 took time to write and wrap up. But it was the best of the series. The mystery's all told, it was just time to say Goodbye for Gabriel.

I wanted to revisit his journey and show him and you, how far he's come at that time. I created the Zolodian race to explain the misconception of the Gods. Where they came from and how the entire structure came to be.

Finally showing Gabriel's rise to be the Phoenix. He 1st finds the real God and follows the words. His abilities reach an all new level and the 1st sign of his bird form.

I loved the challenges to the storyline, I had many versions planned for most scenes in the books. But what was written ended up being the best.

The final battle was to bring the entire struggle to its epic close. The oddest lead up you can think of, and the show of Planet Olympus. And the best fight in the series.

Phoenix 5 is about his lives. Where has he been, what has she done. It's to say goodbye to the storyline. And the end of the Phoenix decade.

I hope you enjoyed reading it as much as I enjoyed writing it!

Phoenix series map out

The Untold Mystery of the Phoenix

The Untold Mystery of the Phoenix 2 Shared Destinies

Freedom Bound

Untold Phoenix 3 Time trials of the Phoenix

Phoenix 4 the end of a Journey

www.ingramcontent.com/pod-product-compliance
Lightning Source LLC
Chambersburg PA
CBHW060920130726
48001CB00006B/2329

* 9 7 9 8 8 3 1 3 0 8 3 4 1 *